Fast Facts About Dogs

Fast Facts About
LABRADOR
RETRIEVERS

by Marcie Aboff

PEBBLE
a capstone imprint

Pebble Emerge is published by Pebble, an imprint of Capstone.
1710 Roe Crest Drive
North Mankato, Minnesota 56003
www.capstonepub.com

Library of Congress Cataloging-in-Publication Data is available on the Library of Congress website.
ISBN 978-1-9771-2450-0 (library binding)
ISBN 978-1-9771-2493-7 (eBook PDF)

Summary: Calling all Labrador retriever fans! Ever wondered about a Labrador retriever's personality? Want to find out the best way to care for a Labrador retriever? Kids will learn all about Labrador retrievers with fun facts, beautiful photos, and an activity.

Image Credits
Capstone Press/Karon Dubke, 20; Getty Images/Smith Collection/Gado, 19; iStockphoto/AtomStudios, 15; Shutterstock: 279photo Studio, back cover, Annette Shaff, 11, BW Folsom, cover (left), el-ka, 18, FREEDOMPIC, 12, Gordon Mackinnon, 16, khrystyna boiko, 4, Kirk Geisler, 9, Natalia Fedosova, cover, NotarYES, 17, Radomir Rezny, 7, stocksre, 5, Susan Schmitz, 6, Vladimir Staykov, 13

Artistic elements: Shutterstock: Anbel, Vector Tradition

Editorial Credits
Editor: Megan Peterson; Designer: Sarah Bennett; Media Researcher: Kelly Garvin; Production Specialist: Tori Abraham

All internet sites appearing in back matter were available and accurate when this book was sent to press.

Printed in the United States of America.
3342

Table of Contents

Words in **bold** are in the glossary.

The Lovable Lab

The Labrador retriever is a lovable dog.
Labs are happy to be part of a family.
They are friendly to people and other dogs.
Labs are the most popular dog **breed**.

Labs make great pets. They are playful and smart. They like to run and swim. Throw a ball to a Lab. The Lab will bring the ball back to you!

A Lab's fur can be yellow, black, or brown. Labs have a **double coat**. The topcoat is rough. The bottom coat is soft and thick. Their fur keeps them warm in cold weather.

Labs are big dogs. They weigh 55 to 80 pounds (25 to 36 kilograms). They stand 22 to 24 inches (56 to 60 centimeters) tall. They are about the same size as the Chesapeake Bay retriever.

Lab History

The first Labs came from Canada. Labs **fetched** ducks for hunters. They helped bring in fishing nets. Years later, people in England raised Labs. They brought Labs to the United States in the early 1900s.

Lab Talents

Labs have many talents. They are great swimmers. They have webbing between their toes. This webbing helps them swim. Labs have wide tails like an otter. The tail swishes back and forth. It helps them turn quickly when swimming.

webbing

Some Labs work as **service dogs**. They are trained to help their owners. Labs help people who are blind. They lead them around busy places. They help them cross streets.

Labs also make good rescue dogs. Labs can find people who are lost. They save people who are hurt. Labs have a strong sense of smell. They follow a person's scent.

Keeping Labs Healthy

Labs are a playful and healthy breed. They still need to visit the **veterinarian** yearly. A vet takes care of animals. They help keep them healthy. The vet will check a Lab's eyes, ears, lungs, and heart. Labs live about 10 to 12 years.

Caring for Labs

Labs are the life of the party! They have a lot of **energy**. They need **exercise** every day. Puppies need to be trained. An untrained Lab might chew up your shoes!

Labs like to eat. Sometimes they eat too much! Be careful not to overfeed your Lab. Brush your Lab every day. They shed a lot. Their teeth should also be brushed daily. Use a dog toothbrush and toothpaste.

Fun Facts About Labs

- One **litter** of Lab puppies can have all three fur colors.

- Labs jump off docks into the water. This dog sport is called dock diving.

- Former president Bill Clinton had a pet Lab named Buddy.

- A Lab was the first dog on the cover of *Life* magazine.

- Labs are not good watch dogs. They are too friendly to strangers!

Make a Dog Toy

What You Need:

- scissors
- about a 1/2 yard (0.5 meter) of cloth
- an old ball, such as a tennis ball
- a piece of ribbon

What You Do:

1. Cut the cloth into two equal strips. Lay the strips in an X on the floor.

2. Set the ball in the center of the X. Fold the strips in half around the ball.

3. Tie the ribbon tightly around the cloth at the base of the ball.

4. Cut the tails of the cloth into many strips.

5. Braid the strips together. Tie knots at the end of the braids with extra cloth.

Glossary

breed (BREED)—a certain kind of animal within an animal group

double coat (DUH-buhl KOHT)—a coat that is thick and soft close to the skin and covered with lighter, silky fur on the surface

energy (EH-nuhr-jee)—the strength to do active things without getting tired

exercise (EK-suhr-syz)—a physical activity done in order to stay healthy and fit

fetch (FECH)—to go after something and bring it back

litter (LIT-ur)—a group of animals born at the same time to the same mother

service dog (SUR-viss DAWG)—a dog trained to help a person who is disabled

veterinarian (vet-ur-uh-NAYR-ee-uhn)—a doctor trained to take care of animals

Read More

Buller, Laura. *Amazing Dogs*. New York: DK Publishing, 2016.

Casteel, Seth. *It's a Puppy's Life*. Washington, D.C.: National Geographic, 2018.

Kenan, Tessa. *I Love Dogs*. Minneapolis: Lerner Publications, 2017.

Internet Sites

American Kennel Club: Labrador Retriever
https://www.akc.org/dog-breeds/labrador-retriever/

Animal Planet
http://www.animalplanet.com/breed-selector/dog-breeds/sporting/labrador-retriever.html

Kiddle: Labrador Retrievers
https://kids.kiddle.co/Labrador_Retriever

Index